To Marcus Pfister, with thanks for all his help
and encouragement. —R.S.

Copyright © 1999 by Nord-Süd Verlag AG, Gossau Zürich, Switzerland
First published in Switzerland under the title *Keine Bange liebe Schlange*
English translation copyright © 1999 by North-South Books Inc.

All rights reserved.
No part of this book may be reproduced or utilized in any form
or by any means, electronic or mechanical, including photocopying,
recording, or any information storage and retrieval system,
without permission in writing from the publisher.

First published in the United States, Great Britain, Canada,
Australia, and New Zealand in 1999 by North-South Books,
an imprint of Nord-Süd Verlag AG, Gossau Zürich, Switzerland.

Distributed in the United States by North-South Books Inc., New York.

Library of Congress Cataloging-in-Publication Data is available.
A CIP catalogue record for this book is available from The British Library.

ISBN 0-7358-1103-2 (trade binding)
3 5 7 9 TB 10 8 6 4 2
ISBN 0-7358-1104-0 (library binding)
1 3 5 7 9 LB 10 8 6 4 2
Printed in Belgium

For more information about our books,
and the authors and artists who create them,
visit our web site: http://www.northsouth.com

Never Fear, Snake My Dear!

Rolf Siegenthaler

Translated by J. Alison James

North-South Books / New York / London

Another dull day in the reptile house. The huge snake tried to recall how long she'd been locked up in this cage. It was so small she could never get unlooped. She longed to be stretched out on a leafy branch, soaking up the sun, dining on succulent rodents.

The only thing she had to look forward to was her ration of three tiny mice per day. They were small, but sweet, and for the few moments it took her to swallow them, she forgot her misery.

So she ignored her aches and dreamed of her homeland, a little island far off in the sea.

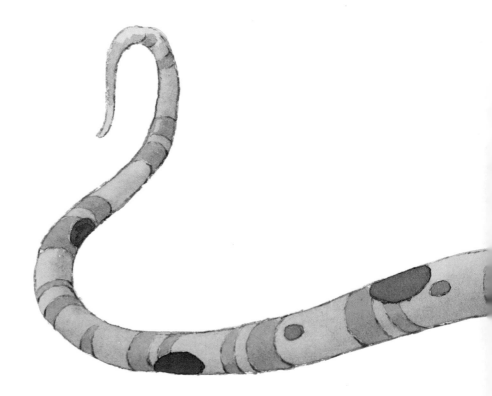

A squeaking noise woke her from her daydream. The roof of her cage was opened, and her dinner mouse dropped right into her mouth.

But before she could swallow it . . .

"Stop! Wait!" screamed the little mouse.

The snake almost choked from shock.

The mouse forced the snake's massive jaws open with all her strength.

"If you spare my life," the mouse gasped, "I'll help you escape from this prison."

The snake shook so much from laughter that the mouse fell out of her mouth onto the ground. "You want to help me?" she asked.

"There's nothing to laugh about," said the mouse. "If you promise not to eat me, I will dig us an underground tunnel to freedom!"

It can't hurt to try, thought the snake. In any case, she wasn't terribly hungry. And if the mouse couldn't do what she promised, well, the snake could always eat her later.

"All right, I agree," said the snake.

"Never fear, Snake my dear," the mouse said confidently. "I'll have us out of here in no time." She began to dig as fast as she could.

Deeper and deeper the hole grew. All night she dug, and in the wee hours of the morning, the tunnel was actually finished. Under the safety of darkness, the two escaped to freedom.

Outside a cat curiously watched the ground bump and wiggle. Soon a mouse will come out, he thought, and I'll snap up a juicy dinner.

But when out popped a wild two-headed monster, the cat bolted like lightning.

"Did you see that scaredy-cat? Me, a wee mouse, inspired mortal terror in a cat!" And she began to sing, "Who's afraid of a little tiny mouse, a little tiny mouse, a little tiny mouse?"

The two laughed heartily and celebrated their newfound freedom.

They slid into the surrounding woods and spent the whole day sleeping in a hollow log. After all her hard work, the little mouse was exhausted. She slept deeply until late afternoon, when she was awakened by the snake.

"I'm terribly hungry," said the snake. "Now I've missed two mouse-meals!"

The mouse saw the greedy look in the snake's eyes and was instantly wide awake. "Never fear, Snake my dear! I'll find us something to eat. In the meantime, tie a knot in your belly. It might help."

They made their way to a nearby city. "Wait here for me," whispered the mouse. "I'll be right back."

When she came back, she was loaded down with a pear, a lemon, a banana, and a piece of cheese.

"I hope you like fruit," she said.

The snake gulped down everything at once.

"Well, you're a good friend," complained the mouse. "The fruit was for you, but I'd hoped for a nibble of the cheese!"

"Oh, don't go on so," said the snake, grinning. "Tie a knot in your belly. It might help."

The mouse had no choice but to go back. But when she returned, her mouth filled with cheese, she was squeaking excitedly, "Let's go! Someone saw me that time."

So the snake whipped herself around into a wheel, the mouse held on, and off they went.

The two rolled and tumbled all the way down a long hill.

Suddenly the snake stopped in her tracks. "Where are we? What is this? Something smells familiar."

"This is the port. You smell the ocean," explained the mouse.

"I remember," said the snake slowly. "I came here five years ago. A ship brought me with other animals from my island. I was terribly homesick." She sniffed. "It seems I still am," she said.

The mouse pondered. Then she said, "If a ship brought you here, then maybe one will take you back. Let's get up somewhere high so we can see all the ships. Perhaps we'll be lucky and you will recognize the one that brought you here. And maybe, if we're really lucky, it will still sail the same route!"

The two looked at all the ships below them.

"It was so long ago," said the snake. "And it's hard to tell in this light, but that small ship over there might be the right one."

"Let's give it a try," said the mouse. "Come on, what are you waiting for?"

"There's no way they'll let us go along!"

"Never fear, Snake my dear! We'll just go as stowaways!"

"And where will you hide me, you know-it-all? I am not a tiny mouse who can tuck into any little crack!"

"I've got a plan. Help me get aboard. And hurry up, so no one sees us!"

"What now?" hissed the snake anxiously.

"Now you lie down here on the deck and roll up tightly. Then everyone will think you're a coil of rope."

And that's just how they did it. The mouse tucked herself in the middle of the coiled snake.

In the dusky early morning, the ship suddenly came to life. Sailors ran here and there. Ropes were fetched, sails hoisted, and the anchor lifted.

The ship set a course for the open sea.

No one noticed that one of the ropes looked very different from the others.

For two days the ship sailed across the high seas.

"When will we ever get there?" asked the snake. "I don't know if I'll be able to move again. I'm so stiff from lying still."

"Never fear, Snake my dear! Surely we'll be there soon."

And shortly after that, a sailor called down from the mast, "Land ho!"

Carefully the snake peeked over the railing. Suddenly she began to hiss excitedly. "That is my island, little mouse! My island! Hold on tight—we're swimming ashore!"

"Isn't this paradise?" asked the snake. She let her long snake belly dangle down from a branch, and the mouse swung on it as if it were a hammock.

"Yes, it's wonderful," agreed the mouse. "Just imagine . . . If you'd eaten me in the zoo, you would never have returned to your island."

"How right you are," answered the snake. "To show my gratitude, I will now become a fruit-eating snake. I'll never ever eat a mouse again."

And so the two unlikely friends lived together happily ever after.